This
Little Tiger book
BeLONgS To:

_____

_____

_____

_____

For Heather,
Erin and Isaac
— AB

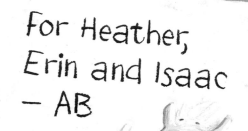

VISIT
GOLDEN
DODO
ZOO
TODAY

LITTLE TIGER PRESS
1 The Coda Centre,
189 Munster Road,
London SW6 6AW
www.littletiger.co.uk

First published in Great Britain 2014
This edition published 2014
Text and illustrations copyright © Alison Brown 2014
Alison Brown has asserted her right to be
identified as the author and illustrator of
this work under the Copyright, Designs and
Patents Act, 1988
A CIP catalogue record for this book is available
from the British Library
All rights reserved • Printed in China
ISBN 978-1-84895-896-8 • LTP/1800/0886/0314
10 9 8 7 6 5 4 3 2 1

Mighty mo

Alison Brown

LITTLE TIGER PRESS
London

Mo was bored.

Bored, bored, bored.

"There must be SOMETHING amazing I can do," Mo said.

Ernestine was making incredible ice creams. "That's IT!" cried Mo. "I can do that!"

"I'll be **MARVELLOUS Mo** — **King** of **Sprinkles!**"

"Triple Whippy, coming up!"

sNAp!

Alphonse was brilliant with balloons.

"I can do THAT. They'll call me

MAGNIFICENT Mo Power-puffer!"

"OOPS!"

"Oh, No, No, No!
Too MUCH
Puff!"

At last Mo found the PERFECT thing.

"Now this looks totally fabulous!" he said.

"I'll be Mo the Majestic

– HAIRDO HERO!"

"Slow down, Mo!"

"GRRRR. NO, MO!"

"Oh."

"I'm not coming out again. EVER!"

"Don't give up, Mo," said his friends. "You'll find SOMETHING SPECIAL to do!" Just at that moment they heard a commotion . . .

"HELP!
HELP!"

"What's the panic, Percival?" asked Mo.
"Big Ron has stolen the Golden Dodo!"
Percival squeaked. "We need YOU, Mo!"

"ME? Why me?"

"You're **super-strong!**
You're **super-fast!**"
cried Percival. "Only YOU
can catch Big Ron!"

"Fantastic!" said Mo. "At last!
Something amazing I can do!"

OTCHA!"

"Put me down!"
Big Ron yelled.

And so Mo did
just that . . .

... right into a BIG pile of elephant poo!

"My lovely robbery - RUINED!" Big Ron blubbed.

"You're nothing but a rotten raccoon!"

Mo smiled. "I'm not just ANY raccoon ..." he said. "I'm Mo ..."

More **MARVELLOUS** and **MAGNIFICENT** books

from Little Tiger Press!

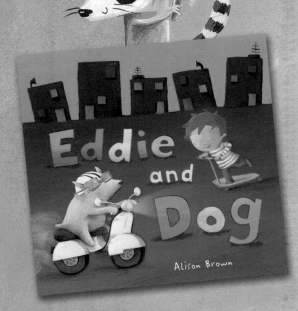

Eddie and Dog

Alison Brown

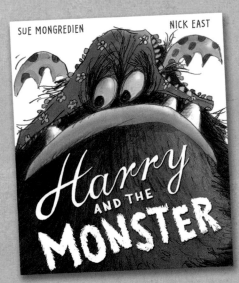

SUE MONGREDIEN NICK EAST

Harry AND THE MONSTER

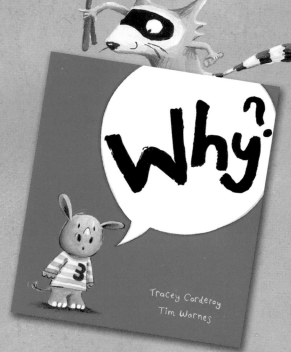

Why?

Tracey Corderoy
Tim Warnes

Jane Chapman
Tim Warnes

Hands off MY HONEY!

Catherine Rayner

Abigail

BIG BAD

STEVE SMALLMAN
RICHARD WATSON

For information regarding any of the above titles
or for our catalogue, please contact us:
Little Tiger Press, 1 The Coda Centre,
189 Munster Road, London SW6 6AW
Tel: 020 7385 6333 • E-mail: contact@littletiger.co.uk
www.littletiger.co.uk